Zebedee's Zoo

Giles Milton
Katharine McEwen

Zebedee's Zoo

ORCHARD BOOKS

In Zebedee's zoo
    every hour of the day
  the mandrill
       dreams
         his
           life
             away.

FEEDING TIMES

7am, 1pm, 6pm

The koalas are snuggled, the cobras yawn,

the cheetahs and tigers have been snoozing since dawn.

A sigh from the lion,
the hippo is snoring,
the zoo by day
is a little bit boring.

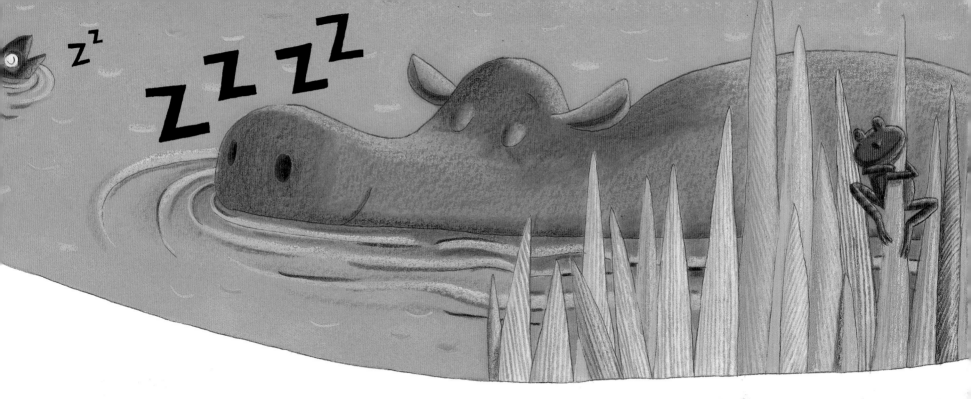

But at seven in the evening,
when Zebedee
leaves . . .

HOoo

. . . there's a shout
from the monkeys up in the trees:

"He's gone! Wake up!
It's almost dark."

oOoK

EEK

PRARK

It's **party** time
in the animal park!

"Switch on the music, hang out the balloons, put on your face paint, hey, wake the baboons!"

Presents and ribbons
and a smart
party dress—
the penguin's a fireman,
the frog's a princess.

EEEK

There's a party
for someone
every night of the week,
tonight it's the llamas
who are having a treat.

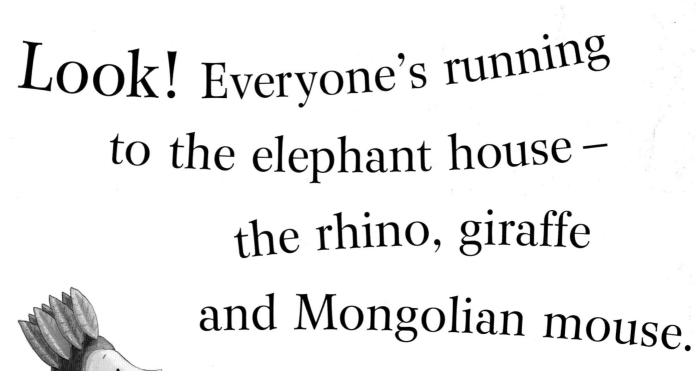

Look! Everyone's running
to the elephant house –
the rhino, giraffe
and Mongolian mouse.

The clock boings midnight
and in Zebedee's house,
not a sound to be heard –
it's as quiet as a mouse.

z^Z^z

BOING

Zebedee dreams
of his animals
all snuggled up warm,
unaware that each night
they party till dawn.

In the elephant bathtub,
eating tons of bananas,

there's a giggling group
of partying llamas.

Turn up
the volume
for the boogying bears,

the pandas are playing
at musical chairs.

The gorilla is patting
and rubbing his belly
as he sucks **up** a bowlful
of strawberry jelly.

Trumpeting elephants,
      the brass band of the zoo:
"Happy Birthday, dear llamas.
                    Happy Birthday,
                    to you!"

There's a shout
from the penguins,
they've got something to say:
"Quick!

Turn off the music!
It's almost day."

HONK

Zebedee's birds and beasts hurry back to their beds . . .

and all day long
rest their weary heads.

So, children,
if you want to
visit the zoo . . .

PWARK

...go there at night – from ten until two!

For John, who likes parties, and Marina, who likes penguins
G. M.

For wee Angus, with love
K. M.

ORCHARD BOOKS
338 Euston Road, London NW1 3BH
Orchard Books Australia
Level 17/207, Kent Street, Sydney, NSW 2000

First published by Orchard Books in 2009
First published in paperback in 2010

Text © Giles Milton 2009
Illustrations © Katharine McEwen 2009
The rights of Giles Milton to be identified as the author and of Katharine McEwen
to be identified as the illustrator of this Work have been asserted by them in
accordance with the Copyright, Designs and Patents Act, 1988.

A CIP catalogue record of this book is available from the British Library.

ISBN: 978 1 40830 432 7

2 4 6 8 10 9 7 5 3 1

Printed in China

Orchard Books is a division of Hachette Children's Books,
an Hachette UK company.
www.hachette.co.uk